The Night Before MOTHER'S DAY

For my mom, Paula Lazutin—N.W.
To my children—I'm so proud of you!—A.W.

ISBN 978-0-545-37232-9

Text copyright © 2010 by Natasha Wing.
Illustrations copyright © 2010 by Amy Wummer.
All rights reserved. Published by Scholastic Inc., 557 Broadway, New York, NY 10012,
by arrangement with Grosset & Dunlap, a division of Penguin Young Readers Group,
a member of Penguin Group (USA) Inc. SCHOLASTIC and associated logos are
trademarks and/or registered trademarks of Scholastic Inc.

12 11 10 9   14 15 16/0

Printed in the U.S.A.   40

First Scholastic printing, April 2011

The Night Before MOTHER'S DAY

By Natasha Wing • Illustrated by Amy Wummer

SCHOLASTIC INC.
New York Toronto London Auckland
Sydney Mexico City New Delhi Hong Kong

'Twas the night before Mother's Day
when, as quiet as a mouse,
Dad told us his plan
to get Mom out of the house.

Her sneakers were set by the doorway with care

in hopes that her running pals soon would be there.

Then out in the yard
there arose quite a crowd.

"Come on! Let's go, girl!"
her friends shouted real loud.

So Mom in her sweat suit and red baseball cap
plugged in her earphones . . .

and *jogged* off in a snap.

Away to the kitchen we flew like a flash

as if we were running a one-hundred-yard dash!

We measured and mixed
a delicious cake batter,

then blended the frosting—oops!
Way too much splatter!

We made fancy cards
adding our "I Love Yous,"

and a special coupon
that Mom sure could use.

When Mom came home, she saw the mess in the sink.

"What'd I miss?"
she asked.
"Nothing," Dad said
with a wink.

We children then nestled
all snug in our beds,
while visions of Mom
danced in our heads.

The next morning we presented a giant bouquet.

"It's for you, Mom!" we cried. "Happy Mother's Day!"

She read both of our cards and, after wiping her eyes, said, "A private spa session! What a lovely surprise."

We took Mom to the kitchen where our spa was set up. Dad served her black coffee in an extra large cup.

We rubbed her shoulders.
We massaged her feet.
Mom sighed and smiled.
"You kids are so sweet."

I wrapped a towel turban
to cover her hair,
then we dabbed on a mud mask.
No mess anywhere!

I painted her nails.
What glittery fun!
A top coat of polish—
voilà! Manicure done!

Dad said, "The chef will be serving a divine gourmet brunch."
(That's a meal that comes between breakfast and lunch.)

So Mom hurried off
to go and get dressed.
We took seats at the table,
behaving our best.

When what to our wondering eyes should appear—
but the perfect model for Mother of the Year!

Her eyes—
how they sparkled!
Her brown hair—
how curly!
Her cheeks were
like roses,
her skirt—
very twirly!

We raised our juice glasses
and offered a toast:
"To the World's Greatest Mom!
And that's not a boast."

Mom thanked us for everything—
it brought her such cheer.
She wished it could be Mother's Day
every day of the year.